THOSE W...
DO . .

Brian instantly drove around the off-balance coach and scored the easy layup.

"Way to toast him!" Dave crowed.

"But use the left next time," MJ couldn't keep himself from adding.

"*What?*" Brian demanded.

"You took the layup with your right hand," MJ explained matter-of-factly. "You should use your left hand when you drive to the left."

"At least I *made* the layup," Brian replied, "which is better than you could do, you klutz!"

"MJ's right," Will said to Brian. "Drive left, shoot with your left hand."

"Yes, sir!" Brian said sarcastically.

MJ felt like a fool. There he was, the worst player on the team, shooting his mouth off. He always knew too much, and said too much.

And it was always Will who stuck up for him.

IN THE
ZONE

by
Hank Herman

BANTAM BOOKS
NEW YORK · TORONTO · LONDON · SYDNEY · AUCKLAND

RL 2.6, 007-010

IN THE ZONE
A Bantam Book / July 1997

Produced by Daniel Weiss Associates, Inc.
33 West 17th Street
New York, NY 10011.

Cover art by Jeff Mangiat.

All rights reserved.

Copyright © 1997 by Daniel Weiss Associates, Inc., and
Hank Herman.

Cover art copyright © 1997 by Daniel Weiss Associates, Inc.
No part of this book may be reproduced or transmitted
in any form or by any means, electronic or mechanical,
including photocopying, recording, or by any information
storage and retrieval system, without permission in
writing from the publisher.
For information address: Bantam Books.

If you purchased this book without a cover you should be aware
that this book is stolen property. It was reported as "unsold and
destroyed" to the publisher and neither the author nor the publisher has
received any payment for this "stripped book."

ISBN: 0-553-48475-3
Published simultaneously in the United States and Canada

Bantam Books are published by Bantam Books, a division of Bantam
Doubleday Dell Publishing Group, Inc. Its trademark, consisting of the
words "Bantam Books" and the portrayal of a rooster, is Registered in U.S.
Patent and Trademark Office and in other countries. Marca Registrada.
Bantam Books, 1540 Broadway, New York, New York 10036.

PRINTED IN THE UNITED STATES OF AMERICA

OPM   0 9 8 7 6 5 4 3 2

To Dewey, a loyal fan

CHAPTER 1

David Danzig dribbled the ball non-chalantly at the top of the key with his right hand. His long blond hair was blowing in the early spring breeze. He had his left hand in the air, with four fingers up.

He's signaling for the play where Derek Roberts gets the open jumper, MJ Jordan realized instantly. He was always able to recognize which sequence was being called quicker than anyone else on the team.

The Bulls were practicing on a small blacktop court in Jefferson

1

Park, an open space full of trees, a lake, and a playground in the middle of the town of Branford. Today it was the Bulls starters against the coaches and subs. MJ was one of the subs. The starters were working on their set plays. The subs, on defense, were supposed to play dumb, as if they weren't familiar with the plays that were being run.

MJ just couldn't seem to do that.

As soon as he noticed Dave's four fingers go up, MJ automatically saw the play unfolding in his mind. Derek, the slim forward he happened to be guarding, would run behind a screen set by two teammates. Then he'd receive a pass from Dave and, *bang,* take the open jumper.

MJ knew all of this was going to happen—and he wasn't supposed to think about it? How could he not? His father had once told him a joke about this very subject. "Whatever you do," Mr. Jordan had said, "don't think about a pink elephant." How could you possibly *not* think about a pink elephant after hearing that?

MJ adjusted his white sports goggles and yanked up the sleeves of his nylon purple-and-gold Lakers windbreaker.  All the other members of the Branford Bulls were hard-core Chicago Bulls fans. MJ had moved to Branford from Los Angeles the summer before and hadn't been able to cut his ties with the Lakers just yet. It was one of MJ's many constant reminders that he wasn't quite like the others on the team.

As he watched Dave, in his long, baggy shorts, lazily yo-yoing the ball, waiting for the play to develop, MJ thought, *Why can't I be more like him?* In MJ's mind, Dave had it all. He was good-looking, funny, popular—and a *born* basketball player. Dave never seemed to have to learn anything; it just came naturally to him. *If* Dave *was guarding Derek*, MJ thought, *he sure wouldn't be worrying about what play was coming up!*

Derek had begun to move to his left. MJ realized if he stayed with him, he'd run smack into the screen and be out of the play. Why should he do that? Derek was about an inch taller than he was and about ten times better! Why just hand him the open jumper?

MJ began chasing Derek, but then instead of following him, he changed direction and waited for Derek to emerge from behind the double screen. Derek received the pass from Dave—but, to his surprise, found MJ all over him.

Mark Fisher, a second-string guard who'd been covering Jo Meyerson at the foul line, dashed over to double-team

Derek. The coaches had taught the Bulls to do that whenever they saw the man with the ball in trouble. MJ and Mark windmilled their arms wildly in front of Derek's face. "Looks like you're dead meat," Mark chirped. The team wise guy, Mark seldom kept his mouth closed for more than a minute at a time.

Derek faked, pivoted, and finally forced up an off-balance jumper that barely hit the rim. Although he was the best player on the team—probably in the *league*—even *Derek* couldn't make a shot with four hands in his face.

Chunky Schwartz, the Bulls beefy, lumbering backup center, reached up and grabbed the rebound for the

subs. Jim Hopwood, one of the Bulls' two teenage coaches, whistled the play dead.

As Chunky handed the ball to Jim,

MJ sidled over to Derek. "You could have kicked the ball out to Jo instead of trying to shoot over the double-team, you know," MJ suggested innocently. "After Mark came over to help me cover you, Jo was wide open."

Jo, the only girl on the Bulls and the only female starter in the Danville County Basketball League, nodded in agreement. Derek nodded his head up and down, as if to say, *Guess you're right*. Talented as he was, Derek didn't mind taking a suggestion if it was a good one. But MJ knew the nod was about as much of a response as he could expect. Derek never spoke unless it was absolutely necessary.

The look MJ got from Jim, however, was not quite so pleasant. "How are we supposed to run our plays if you screw them up like that?" Jim demanded, staring down at MJ. "I know *you* know all the plays, but you're supposed to pretend you don't know what's coming, remember?"

"I couldn't help it, Coach," MJ answered feebly.

"Well *try* to help it," Jim snapped. Then he turned his back on MJ. "All right, Dave. Set up the offense again. Let's go!"

MJ felt tempted to defend himself further, but he knew it would be useless. Jim considered him a know-it-all and had resented him right from the start. MJ sometimes got the feeling that Jim thought he was the only one who was supposed to understand the game of basketball!

Jim had tossed the ball to Dave to trigger a new play. Dave shook the hair out of his eyes and held the ball with two hands over his head. But this time, instead of calling out a play, he simply skidded a hard bounce pass to Will Hopwood, Jim's younger brother, who was playing the high post. Will, the Bulls' tall, dark-haired center, was well covered by Chunky. Without hesitation, Will rifled the ball right back to Dave.

Smart move, MJ thought approvingly. *Will's the only kid on the team who knows as much about basketball as I do . . . and he sure plays it a whole lot better!* It was at times like this that MJ really regretted that his parents had named him Michael Jordan. *How can someone with that name be as uncoordinated as I am?* he thought miserably.

Jim was crouched down in front of Dave, guarding him closely. Dave had his knees flexed, and he had his two hands on the ball, slightly to the right of his body, in the triple-threat position: ready to shoot, pass, or dribble.

But MJ knew that one way or another, Dave was going to try to score. Jim was a co-captain of the Branford High varsity basketball team, as was Nate Bowman, Jr., the other Bulls coach. *All* the Bulls—and Dave, especially—loved nothing more than schooling their hot-shot coaches.

MJ wasn't surprised to see Dave go into his trademark slow-motion dribble:

left to right to left to right, back and forth, over and over again, as if he were trying to lull his defender to sleep. Then he dribbled the ball through his legs and tried a little shake-and-bake routine.

While Dave was busy showing off all his moves, the always-hustling Will got away from Chunky and sliced through the lane. But Dave didn't get him the ball. He never even saw him.

Even though MJ was playing *against* Dave, he *hated* to see that kind of missed opportunity.

"Gotta keep your head up, Droopy," he advised, using Dave's nickname. "Gotta see the floor. Will was wide open."

Dave didn't answer, but MJ felt the point guard's stare cutting through him like a steak knife. Everyone knew Dave Danzig was one of the coolest kids in the fifth grade, and when he wanted to make you feel like two cents, he sure could do it.

When Dave finished staring down MJ, he looked over at Brian Simmons, the small forward, and snickered. MJ was aware that the two best friends both thought of him as a stiff who knew too much about hoops for his own good. Maybe he shouldn't have said anything. . . . *But it was such a dumb play!*

MJ noticed that it was beginning to get a little too dark out to see, and the blacktop at Jefferson had no lights. He was also starting to feel pretty chilly, even with his Lakers windbreaker. On these early spring days, it always seemed nice and warm right after school, but when the sun went down, it felt more like winter again.

"Last five minutes," Jim announced. "A couple more plays, Dave."

Dave started the play from halfcourt, throwing a chest pass to Brian. MJ didn't envy Brian: Being guarded by Nate Bowman was no picnic. Nate was widely considered the best highschool basketball player in the county. And even though he sometimes went easy on the younger boys in practice, every once in a while he liked to leap high in the air for a dramatic rejection—showing the Bulls who's "the man." He especially enjoyed swatting away Brian's specialty shot, his fadeaway jumper.

All the Bulls knew this, including Brian, and it wasn't long before Brian gave Nate a little pump fake. Sure enough, Nate went soaring into the air. Brian instantly drove around the off-balance coach and, with a big grin on his face, scored the easy layup.

"Way to toast him!" Dave crowed.

"But use the left next time," MJ couldn't keep himself from adding.

Brian, dark eyes blazing, shot him a deadly look. "*What?*" he demanded.

"You took the layup with your right hand," MJ explained matter-of-factly. "You should use your left hand when you drive to the left. The coaches always tell us that. Especially in practice, when it doesn't really matter if you miss."

The more MJ spoke, the more self-conscious he felt. All eyes were on him, and he noticed the whole team had gotten very, very quiet.

Brian slowly ran his hand through his fade haircut, taking his time to reply.

"You're trying to tell *me* to use my left hand?" he asked finally, in a menacing tone. "At least I *made* the layup—which is better than you could do, you klutz!"

MJ tried hard to swallow. He noticed Dave winking at Brian. Chunky and Mark were both stifling giggles.

MJ could tell that Jo, Derek, and Nate were embarrassed for him by their sheepish expressions, but nobody spoke up in his behalf.

Except for Will.

"MJ's right," Will said finally to Brian. "And you know it. Drive left, shoot with your left hand."

Brian smirked, then snapped Will a mock-salute. "Yes, sir!" he said sarcastically.

MJ felt like a fool. There he was, the worst player on the team, shooting his mouth off. He always knew too much, and said too much.

And it was always Will who stuck up for him.

CHAPTER 2

Will felt just about as comfortable as he could get. His right leg was draped over the back of the Danzigs' tan living room couch, and his left hand was resting on the edge of a large bowl of potato chips. His only job was to lay back and do the play-by-play as Brian and Dave madly clicked their controllers in a game of NBA Live 97.

"Joe Dumars dribbles to the top of the key for Detroit," Will announced, "and he drains the three! Pistons go up, sixty-four to forty-eight."

"Too-Tall? Fadeaway? David? Need any more chips or iced tea?" Dave's mother offered.

"No thanks, Mrs. D.," Brian answered automatically, still clicking away feverishly. Will realized Brian hadn't really heard the question. He was too intent upon trying to make a comeback.

Will was known as Too-Tall because, at five foot four, he was the tallest of the fifth-grade Branford Bulls. Brian was called Fadeaway both because of his fade haircut and his deadly fadeaway jumper. Will knew Mrs. Danzig referred to them by their nicknames to feel more like she was part of the team, but she really didn't have to.

For one thing, she made it to every Bulls game, and they could always hear her cheering wildly. For another, Will and Brian—who along with Dave made up the three original Bulls— just about *lived* at her house, and she was always spoiling them.

On top of that, she was pretty.

Will stopped announcing in order to stuff a handful of chips in his mouth. Dave picked up the play-by-play where Will left off.

"Grant Hill continues to absolutely *kick butt*," he shouted with glee, "and nobody on the Sonics can handle him."

Since all three boys rooted for the Chicago Bulls, there was a gentleman's agreement that none of them could be the Bulls in NBA Live 97. Dave had chosen the Detroit Pistons, since he was a big Grant Hill fan. Brian had taken the Seattle Supersonics.

"Yeah," Will chimed in, his words garbled through a mouthful of chips, "Detroit is pounding Seattle, just like we're gonna crush Rochester tomorrow." The Branford Bulls were scheduled to play the Rochester Ravens, one of the so-so teams in the league, the next day.

"The only decent player they have is Spuds Marinaro," Will continued, "and I guess you guys won't have to worry about him." Will pounded himself on the chest, as if to say, *Marinaro's the center; I'll take care of him myself.*

Brian threw his controller down in frustration as time ran out on his comeback attempt. "Yeah," he added, "just put some tape over your sidekick's mouth, and we'll do just fine. Man, is he annoying!"

Will knew his "sidekick" meant MJ. Before he could respond to Brian, Dave jumped into the conversation. "Is it my imagination," Dave asked, "or is MJ getting worse and worse? He just can't seem to keep his mouth shut—ever! Imagine, *him* telling *me* to keep my head up yesterday!"

Will stared at both of them. "You know, you two guys never learn," he said to Dave and Brian. "It's just like back at All-Star Hoops Camp," Will continued, referring to their adventures the summer before.

Dave rolled his eyes. He'd heard

Will's thoughts on this topic before.

"You two were against MJ right from the start," Will went on, ignoring Dave's response. "You never really liked him. If I remember right, you guys preferred to hang around with *Slick Washington*."

Slick was a cool character from the inner city who'd won Brian and Dave over with his exciting streetwise ways. But he proved himself to be a rotten apple who'd turned on the boys from Branford—and eventually got himself kicked out of camp.

Will often threw this scenario back in their faces at times like this when their judgment was in question.

Brian held his tongue for a few seconds, looking sheepish.

"No, this is different," Brian insisted finally, his dark eyes focused earnestly on Will. "This has nothing to do with liking MJ or not liking MJ. It's just that we already *have* two coaches—and two good ones. The last thing we need is MJ sticking his two cents in every time someone on the team makes a move."

Will weighed what his friend was saying. He knew there was some truth to it. Just as he was getting ready to admit that Brian might have a point, Dave spoke up.

"Besides being a know-it-all," Dave added, "MJ's by far the worst player on the team. Everyone knows the only reason he's on the Bulls is because he kissed up to you at camp last summer."

As soon as the words were out of his mouth, Dave's face turned a bright red. Brian, too, looked shocked.

Will felt like he'd been kicked in the stomach. He had always assumed a lot of the Bulls probably *thought* what Dave had just expressed. But nobody had ever come out and *said* it to his face before.

Yeah, maybe MJ did make the Bulls because he's my friend, Will reluctantly admitted to himself. *But still— he brings something to the team that we really need.*

"Don't you guys understand?" Will asked, frustrated. "MJ sees *everything* that happens on the floor. He's able to explain things that other guys just don't get. He knows this game *inside out!*"

"Yeah," Dave replied, "and he *reminds* everyone how much he knows every chance he gets."

Will shook his head miserably. How could he ever get the rest of the Bulls to appreciate what MJ contributed to the team?

MJ loosened the band on his sports goggles. For some reason they'd felt uncomfortable the whole game, even though they were no tighter than usual.

He glanced down at Mark and Chunky, the other benchwarmers. The generous amount of space they'd deliberately left between themselves and him wasn't lost on MJ.

He looked back at the court in time to see Dave dribble the ball off his foot and out-of-bounds.

It was a pretty unusual turnover for one of the best ball handlers in the league—but that's the way things had been going for the Bulls. They were behind 33–31, late in the third quarter. The fans of the hometown Ravens, smelling an upset, were beginning to whoop it up. In the tiny gym, the thirty or so voices sounded like three hundred.

I wonder what the temperature is in this sweatbox, MJ thought. He looked down at his red jersey with the black number 27 on it. It was drenched with perspiration—and he'd only played two minutes so far, back in the second quarter.

Thinking about it, MJ realized it wasn't just his goggles, or the temperature in the gym, that was making him uncomfortable. When Jim had announced the starting five just prior to the opening tip, he'd added sarcastically, "That sound okay to you, MJ?"

His cutting words still echoed in MJ's mind. *Jim really knows how to hurt a kid*, MJ thought. And it hadn't taken long for some of the Bulls to pick up on their coach's lead.

When Jo had opened the scoring for the Bulls with a jumper after a

sweet pass from Derek, Chunky had tapped MJ on the shoulder. "Hey, MJ," he'd said, "did you see Derek kick it out to Jo on the perimeter, just like you told him to?" Then he'd slapped Mark on the back, and they'd both laughed.

Though MJ knew he shouldn't let those two scrubs bother him, the taunting had made him wince anyway.

And at the start of the second quarter, after Dave made a brilliant no-look pass to Will that brought the Bulls rooters to their feet, the point guard ran by MJ on the bench and asked in a loud voice, "Did I see the floor okay that time, MJ?"

It was obvious to MJ that his "coaching" had become a big topic of nasty conversation behind his back. And since he'd never totally fit in with the Bulls to begin with—always feeling a little like a party crasher—the mocking made him feel doubly self-conscious.

He decided to put a lid on his coaching instincts for a while, even though it went against his nature. The moment the second half had started, MJ had noticed the Ravens were switching from a man-to-man defense to a zone. He'd kept quiet.

Finally, three pos-sessions later, Dave had yelled out, "Zone! They're in a zone. Let's go to our motion offense."

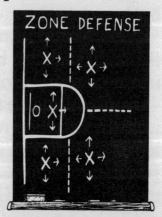

"Good call!" Jim had shouted approv-ingly.

Oh, it's okay if Dave *notices something and tells the team what to do,* MJ had thought resentfully. *It's only out of line if* I'm *the one who speaks up.*

And now here they were, near the end of the third period, down by two to a team they should have run off the court by halftime. Brian was dribbling on the left side of the court, just beyond the three-point circle.

"Isolation!" MJ heard Jim call out. Obviously, the coach figured Brian could take Rowdy Rollins, the Ravens' bowlegged small forward, and wanted to clear the court so Brian could work on him one-on-one.

Brian gave a good fake to his right, and Rowdy went for it. With his defender leaning the wrong way, Brian drove to his left and tossed in the layup with his left hand, tying the score at thirty-three all.

"See that?" he called over to MJ on the Bulls' bench, smirking. "Drive left, shoot left. Works every time."

MJ felt the eyes of all

his teammates on him. *All right, already, I get the point!* MJ thought. *We could be up by fifteen if these guys would stop worrying about dissing me and start playing ball!*

As the fourth quarter began, MJ noticed that Spuds Marinaro, the Ravens' center and top gun, was overplaying Will to the right. Apparently he was so sure Will would only drive right that he was practically *giving* him the left side.

MJ knew he was better off keeping the observation to himself, but if he could only let Will know, it might mean the difference between winning and losing.

Before he realized what he was doing, MJ had popped up off the bench and put his left hand over his right, forming a T. Will, catching the signal from out on the floor, asked the referee for a time-out.

Seeing the Bulls come jogging over in his direction, Jim exploded.

"*Who* called that time-out?" he demanded.

Will looked confused. His face flushed. "I did," he said. "I thought you wanted the time-out. I saw MJ get off the bench and signal—"

"*What?*" Jim thundered, directing his gaze at MJ. "*You* again! Who made *you* the coach? *I'm* the one who calls time-outs on this team—and I wanted to save them for crunch time. Now you've burned one, and for what?"

MJ felt very nervous about standing up to the coach, but he had to defend himself. In a loud voice, he began, "I thought a time-out was important, since Marinaro was overplaying Will to the—"

"Who *cares* what you think?" Jim interrupted, glaring angrily at MJ.

MJ clammed up immediately and stared down at his feet.

Jim went on fuming at MJ until the

buzzer sounded, calling the Bulls back out on the floor.

MJ never even got a chance to make his point about Spuds Marinaro, but he didn't care anymore. He just wished he could crawl under the bleachers and hide. He'd do *anything* to escape the coach's furious gaze.

The Bulls lost by six.

Though MJ knew his calling the time-out had little or nothing to do with the loss, it was clear that Jim didn't see it that way.

Throughout the closing minutes, as the game slipped further out of reach, the riled-up coach kept sputtering about how "We'd be better off without that little know-it-all," and how "That lame time-out killed off any chance for momentum we might have had."

All right, already, MJ thought resentfully, *I think you've made your point!*

As the Bulls were gathering their

warm-up pants and jackets from under the bench, MJ overheard some heated words between Nate and Jim.

"You've got to go easy on him," Nate was saying. "This kid *lives* for the Bulls, and he really knows his hoops. He's contributing in the best way he can."

Jim tried to defend himself, but then MJ heard Will cut him off.

"Face it, Jim, you have a double standard," Will said angrily to his older brother. "If Derek had called for that time-out, you wouldn't be so upset. You just don't like it when MJ speaks up, 'cause he's not one of the more talented players."

MJ backed away. He didn't want to hear any more. Though he appreciated Nate's and Will's support, the last thing he wanted was their pity.

CHAPTER 4

MJ dribbled the ball awkwardly down the uneven sidewalk along Mulberry Avenue on his way to Jefferson Park. He never seemed to get beyond four or five bounces without the ball hitting a crack, or smacking against his knee, or *something*. He wished he could dribble like Dave Danzig. That kid could handle the ball as though it were attached to his hand by a string!

Reaching the stone pillars that marked the entrance to the park, MJ turned down the narrow path that led to the blacktop. He was surprised to hear the birds chirping in the trees; he hadn't realized they were back from their winter vacation. A mild breeze rustled his lightweight Lakers windbreaker. Too bad his mood didn't match the sunny spring weather.

Sunday was not a required practice day, just an informal shoot-around. But on most Sundays—particularly on Sundays following a Bulls loss—the majority of the team tended to show up.

Usually MJ couldn't wait to reach the blacktop, but today he made especially sure he was *not* the first to arrive. He didn't want to appear too eager.

Catching a glimpse of the blacktop through the trees, MJ saw he didn't have to worry. Brian, Dave, Will, Derek, Jo, and Chunky were already there, lazily hoisting up all sorts of shots.

As MJ reached the edge of the blacktop and unzipped his windbreaker, he noticed a strange, sudden quiet. He felt very self-conscious and got the clear sense that the Bulls had been talking about him—again.

To break the ice, Will said, "MJ makes seven. MJ, why don't you ref for a few minutes until Mark gets here."

"I don't think Mark's coming today," Chunky stated as he worked on his turnaround jumper. It was a shot he'd been trying to pick up from Will for the last several months.

"That's okay," MJ said quickly. "I like reffing."

Though he'd never admit it to any of the Bulls, reffing, announcing, analyzing, coaching—those were the parts of basketball he really loved. He couldn't make a fool of himself doing those things, the way he so often did when he *played* the game.

"Yeah, great idea," Dave said of MJ's offer to ref. "That's what you're good at." Dave glanced over at Brian, raising his eyebrows.

Before MJ could figure out what the look meant, Brian said, "Me,

Dave, and Chunky versus the rest of you guys." That meant Will, Derek, and Jo.

Since Derek and Will were the two best all-around players on the Bulls, MJ felt Will's team had a definite advantage. But Brian's team got off to a quick start. Brian himself was on target from his sweet spot on the left side, canning three fadeaway jumpers in a row to get things going.

"Come on, get up on that guy," Will chided Derek jokingly. "That dude can shoot."

"He's in the zone all right!" MJ added excitedly.

Then he saw Dave look at Brian—and both of them broke out laughing. MJ figured out what it was. He knew the two of them made fun of him all the time behind his back about all the basketball jargon he used. And "in the zone" was one of his favorites.

He felt his face flush. No matter what he did, Brian and Dave would find a way to make fun of him.

A slashing layup by Derek cut Brian's team's lead to two baskets. Chunky had the ball in the lane. Closely guarded by Will, he pump-faked a few times before passing out to Brian. But he shuffled his feet just a little bit in the process.

"Travel!" MJ called out instantly, rolling his arms one over the other in a lawn-mower motion to signal the violation.

"What kind of travel?" Chunky asked peevishly, putting both hands on his hips.

"Hey, the refs are cracking down on foot shuffling this year," MJ explained in a patient voice. "You've got to learn that."

"And I guess *you're* the one who's going to teach it," Dave said with a smirk.

MJ caught Will and Jo exchanging concerned looks. But they didn't say anything.

A few plays later, Dave faked a pass to Brian, but in doing so, momentarily lost control of the ball. Quickly regaining possession, he prepared to shoot.

"Violation!" MJ announced. "Can't catch your own pass."

"Oh, get off it, MJ!" Dave said vehemently, waving an arm at him. "It's just a Sunday half-court game. So I fumbled the ball for half a second. Do you *always* have to open your mouth?" His voice was heavy with disgust.

There was a long, uncomfortable silence as Dave shot MJ a hostile glare.

"He's just doing what we asked him to do, man," Derek finally said quietly.

This defense, from the normally wordless forward, meant a lot to MJ. He silently thanked him.

"You're right, Derek," Brian jumped in. "But we asked him to *ref*, not to *coach*. Why does MJ feel he always has to *teach*?" Then he snickered as he asked, "Is he really that much better than all of us?"

"Hey, Fadeaway, give him a break." Now it was Jo sticking up for MJ. "He sees things we don't all see. There's nothing wrong with that. It wouldn't hurt you guys to listen to him once in a while." She was looking at Brian, Dave, and Chunky when she said "you guys."

MJ wasn't at all surprised to find Jo on his side. She knew as well as anyone how it felt to be picked on. When she first joined the team, some of the Bulls hadn't wanted her because she was a girl. Later on, they froze her out for a few games when they thought she was being a ball hog.

"You can look at it any way you

want," Chunky said finally. "The guy's just a pain in the butt."

Throughout the conversation, MJ had been quietly backing farther and farther away from the blacktop. At Chunky's stinging remark, he turned and began walking steadfastly away.

"You guys are really sleazeballs," MJ heard Will spit out at the others behind him.

Then Will went running to head MJ off, as if he were trying to beat his man back downcourt on a fast break.

"These guys are just being jerks," Will huffed, all out of breath, as he faced MJ. "Just let me straighten 'em out and—"

MJ held up his hands, cutting Will off in midsentence. "Thanks, but don't bother. You and I know what they all think of me—and they're probably right. I *do* talk too much."

MJ slammed his basketball down hard on the paved path, as if to emphasize what he was about to say.

"But things are going to change.

From now on, you'll never hear me give another word of instruction, or even make a suggestion. Not in practice. Not in games. *Ever*."

"But—," Will objected.

"I'm serious, Will," MJ insisted. "Hey, listen," he added, trying to close the subject, "I'm heading over to Bowman's. Maybe I'll see you there later."

MJ headed back up the path toward Mulberry Avenue, leaving his friend standing there with his hands outstretched.

In a weird way, MJ had enjoyed making his speech. He'd liked the dramatic sound of what he'd said. But now a panic came over him.

If I can't read the defenses, if I can't make suggestions, if I can't help the coaches coach, then what can *I do?* MJ worried. *My role on this team was pretty small to begin with. If I can't even contribute ideas from the bench, I won't have any role at all!*

CHAPTER 5

Bowman's Market was located on Mulberry Avenue directly across from the entrance to Jefferson Park. But convenience was by no means the only reason the Bulls went to Bowman's for sodas after every practice and every game.

Bowman's was owned and operated by Mr. Nathaniel Bowman, Sr., Nate's dad. Mr. Bowman, or "Mr. B.," as a lot of the Bulls called

him, was a balding, fiftyish widower who had gotten a little heavy around the middle. He also happened to be the strongest Bulls supporter in town. A former standout basketball player himself, Mr. Bowman was the perfect guy to talk to after a tough practice or a tough game.

Will had worried that he wouldn't find MJ at Bowman's, and that MJ's *Maybe I'll see you there later* was just a polite brush-off. But sure enough, Will spotted MJ at the counter, still in his Lakers windbreaker. MJ was so engaged in his conversation with Mr. Bowman that he didn't even seem to notice Will and the rest of the Bulls come in.

Will quickly picked up the gist of the conversation. The tall store owner was telling MJ how he'd been one of the only African Americans in an almost all-white high school. Will had heard the story before.

MJ happened to be an African American, too, but Will knew that wasn't the reason Mr. Bowman was telling him about his own experience. *Somehow* the shopkeeper had already gotten MJ to spill the beans about what was bothering him, and he was using this story to make MJ feel a little better about being the odd man out.

Will marveled. Whenever any of the Bulls felt troubled, Mr. Bowman had an appropriate story. True, his stories sounded kind of corny if you weren't the one with the problem. But if it *was* your problem, what Mr. Bowman had to say was always right on the money.

Dave, noticing MJ at the counter, called out, "Hey, MJ, you should have stayed. We kicked those guys' butts from here to Indiana. And man, was I ever in the zone!"

Saying this, he punched Brian on the shoulder and guffawed. But one stern look from Mr. Bowman wiped the smile off his face.

Everyone knew that Dave was one of Mr. Bowman's favorites. Since Dave's dad had passed away a few years back, Mr. Bowman had been like a father to him. But right now, the store owner was dealing with *MJ's* problem. His look to Dave, Will knew, meant *Zip it!*

At that moment the door to the shop swung open and Jim and Nate flew in. The two tall basketball stars, in their blue-and-white varsity jackets, always looked incredibly cool.

Man, they stomp in here like they own the joint, Will thought. Then he chuckled to himself. *Well, I guess in Nate's case, he can afford to act that way.*

"Hey, Pops, let me guess: I'm just in time to help," Nate said, flashing his trademark broad grin.

All the Bulls laughed. *You're just in time to help* is what Mr. Bowman always said when he laid eyes on his son.

"Matter of fact," Mr. Bowman

began, "I *could* use a little help with—"

"Oh, come on, Pops," Nate cut in. Will saw a flash of sunlight glinting off the seventeen-year-old's gold stud earring. "Gimme a break. It's Sunday. And Jim and I are only staying for a few minutes."

"Sure, drink my soda, then hit the road," Mr. Bowman said, as if he were feeling used. But Will knew it was all in jest. Mr. Bowman was always happy to see Nate, Jim, and the rest of the Bulls—for however long.

Jim scanned the Bulls sitting at the counter. "How'd the shoot-around go?" he asked. Then, spotting MJ, he cracked, "Hey, MJ, teach them anything new today?"

Will saw Mr. Bowman shoot his brother the same kind of deadly, silencing look he'd just beamed at Dave moments earlier. Jim looked surprised, but Will was sure he'd gotten the message.

"So who do you guys have coming up next Saturday?" the shopkeeper asked the group in general. Will could see Mr. Bowman was trying to steer the conversation back to safer ground.

"Sampton!" three or four Bulls shouted at the same time.

"That's right," Mr. Bowman said, as if he were surprised. "The Sampton Slashers! How could I have forgotten that?"

Will was pretty sure Mr. Bowman *hadn't* forgotten but was just making conversation. *Everyone* had their calendars circled for showdowns with the Sampton Slashers. The Slashers, the most obnoxious team in the Danville County Basketball League, were the Bulls' archrivals. Every season, it seemed to be the Bulls and the Slashers fighting it out down to the wire for the top spot. And making matters even more interesting, Jo's brother, Otto Meyerson, was the Slashers' leading player.

Chunky slid his empty can down the counter in Mr. Bowman's direction. The store owner put another

48

cold soda on the counter and slid it over to Chunky. "This one's on me," he said to the fleshy, sweating backup center. "You look like you need it. So you going to tear up those Slashers next Saturday, Chunkster?"

"Count on it!" Chunky replied, popping open the top of his Pepsi. "Well, maybe not me *personally*. You know us scrubs don't always see a lot of playing time in the big games."

Will knew Chunky was saying this for Jim's benefit. While the subs played their share in the majority of the games, Jim tended to rely mostly on his starting five against tough teams like the Slashers and the Portsmouth Panthers. Chunky was constantly lobbying for more playing time.

"Hey, that's okay, that's okay," Mr. Bowman soothed. "You do what you can do. I remember there was this fellow on my college team—a little guy by the name of Ira Shane. There was only one thing he could do really well, and that was shoot free throws."

Mr. Bowman paused, as if he were trying to call up a picture of Ira Shane in his mind. "This guy never got in until the last few minutes of the game, when the other team would start fouling us to stop the clock. Then Coach would send in old Ira, he'd get himself fouled, and then,

boom, he'd make his free throws. Automatic."

Though Mr. Bowman was telling the story to Chunky, Will could see that MJ was hanging on every word. Behind his thick glasses, his eyes were wide open.

"That's really all he ever did?" Chunky asked. "Shoot free throws?"

"All he ever did. Though it wasn't such a bad specialty," Mr. Bowman added, with a twinkle in his eye. "My senior year, we won the championship game by one point. By a free throw. Any idea who made that free throw?"

"Ira Shane?" Chunky volunteered.

"You got it—Ira Shane," Mr. Bowman replied. "He was the original role player. Hey, look, everyone's got his own strengths and weaknesses. You've just got to contribute in any way you can."

Out of the corner of his eye, Will saw MJ's mouth turn up in the tiniest smile. It was the first happy expression he'd seen on his friend's face in days.

Will had to hand it to Mr. Bowman. He'd used Chunky's chance comment about limited playing time to weave this whole long Ira Shane story—and all the time the story was intended to boost *MJ's* spirits. What's more, it had worked!

The guy's a genius, Will thought, shaking his head. He wasn't even sure whether or not the story was true, but he realized it didn't matter.

CHAPTER 6

Now this is one really cool car, Will thought as he scrunched into the backseat of the Jordans' convertible.

Will usually got a ride to games with his older brother, or with Nate in the Bullsmobile—as the Bowman's Market van was known. But 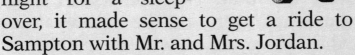 since he'd been at MJ's house Friday night for a sleepover, it made sense to get a ride to Sampton with Mr. and Mrs. Jordan.

A lot of the Bulls complained about having to play all their games on the road, since the town of Branford had no community center gym. But Will didn't mind. Most of the parents came along to watch and cheer anyway, so what was the big deal about the home-court advantage? Besides, he loved the Sampton Community Center gym, with its full-sized floor and glass backboards.

And the Bulls have already won a few critical contests there, he reflected proudly.

"Big game today, huh?" Mrs. Jordan asked from the front passenger seat.

"*All* Bulls-Slashers games are big, Eva," Mr. Jordan commented self-importantly, as if his wife should have known better than to ask something so obvious. He always made it clear that he was up on Bulls basketball. Will had noticed that a lot of parents were like that. They needed to show that they were in the know about what was going on with their kids.

"This game's even bigger than usual," Will volunteered. His parents had often told him not to sit like a bump on a log when other kids' moms or dads were giving him a ride, so he was trying to keep up his end of the conversation. "We're seven-and-three, and so are the Slashers. Portsmouth too. So we're in a three-way tie for first."

After a short stretch of silence, Mrs. Jordan turned around to face her son. "Michael? You're awfully quiet today. Anything the matter?"

MJ didn't answer. He just squirmed in his seat. The quiet was making Will very uncomfortable. Finally, he felt forced to speak for MJ.

"Oh, some of the Bulls have been getting on his case. . . ."

Catching MJ's sudden, fierce look, Will quickly added, "But it's no big deal."

"What are they on your case about, honey?" Mrs. Jordan pursued.

"Never mind," MJ answered through

clenched teeth, glaring at Will.

"Come on, Michael, you can tell your dear old dad," his father prodded, keeping his eyes on the road.

Mr. Jordan's syrupy voice seemed to make MJ burst.

"*Why'd* you have to name me Michael Jordan?" MJ suddenly shouted.

Will almost jumped out of the backseat of the convertible. His friend's explosion had caught him totally off-guard.

"What were you *thinking?*" MJ continued passionately. "Do you have any *idea* how hard it is being a stiff like me and having a name like *Michael Jordan?*"

Will heard MJ's mother gasp. Then both parents rushed to speak at the same time.

"You may not be the best player in town, but you're no stiff," Mr. Jordan said.

"When you were born, Michael Jordan wasn't nearly as famous as he is today," Mrs. Jordan said, her voice overlapping her husband's.

But MJ kept charging ahead, without listening to either of them.

"And these glasses I have to wear all the time! And the ridiculous white goggles for the games! You know what a *jerk* I look like? I don't know *why* we ever had to move to this stupid town from L.A. in the first place!"

"Michael, Michael," his father pleaded, "we've been through that a hundred times. My company—"

But MJ cut him off again.

"And now I'm stuck being the new kid on this stupid team. Everybody else is old buddies. Will and Brian and Dave have known one another just about since they were born! And they all think I'm only on this team because I managed to get friendly with Will."

Will was thankful for the cool breeze blowing in the backseat of the convertible, because things were getting pretty tense.

"MJ," he consoled, "they just *say* that. They all know you belong on the Bulls."

"Oh yeah, sure!" MJ shouted. He was getting more and more hysterical. "Face it, Will. They hate me. They *all* hate me. And now I can't even say anything on the bench, or I'll get blamed for losing the game. Do you know what it's like to see what I see on the court and not even be able to *say* anything?"

Will felt terrible.

"But you *can* speak up, MJ," Will insisted. "You heard what Mr. B. said last Sunday after the shoot-around. About Ira Shane? That everyone has to contribute in any way he can?"

"Oh, come on, Will!" MJ said, giving him a sharp look. "Sure, that made me feel better for a minute. But you know Mr. Bowman. He's always trying to make everyone feel better. But he's not one of the Bulls. He's not one of the ones making fun of me all the time."

Will tried desperately to think of something helpful to say. But he was stuck.

"So what are you going to do?" he asked weakly.

MJ took a deep breath. "It's like I told you last Sunday in Jefferson Park," he answered. "You're never going to hear me say another word to the Bulls. *Never!*"

"Oh, sure," Will said sarcastically. "You're going to take a vow of silence."

"You got it," MJ replied. He sounded totally serious. "A complete vow of silence."

His mother, who'd been listening anxiously the whole time in the front seat, finally ventured, "But isn't that a little extreme, honey?"

MJ didn't answer.

I guess his vow of silence has begun, Will thought grimly.

CHAPTER 7

The Bulls look like they're beginning to drag, MJ thought. *Especially Brian and Dave.* As usual in a Bulls-Slashers game, Jim and Nate had not used the subs much. Chunky had been in for Will for a couple of minutes at the end of the first quarter, when it looked like Will was ready to come to blows with Ratso Renzulli, Sampton's obnoxious center. And Mark had given Jo a two-minute breather at the start of the second quarter when Jo had developed a stitch in her side.

MJ himself hadn't seen any action yet.

The first half had been brutal—
what Jim liked to call "a war." The
pace had been extremely fast, with
both teams pushing the ball up the
floor. Very physical. Every shot well
defended, every pass challenged. MJ
had been surprised by the Slashers:
Normally known as a team interested
only in offense, they had certainly
turned up the defensive pressure on
the Bulls so far.

MJ glanced up at the bleachers
behind the Bulls' bench: rows of red
and dark blue—Bulls rooters loyally
wearing the team's colors. Across
the gym, MJ saw the black and gold
of the Slashers fans. The noise level
in the gym was cranked up so high
that he could barely hear himself
think.

The Slashers had jumped off to a
5–0 lead to start the game on quick
baskets by Ratso Renzulli and point
guard Otto Meyerson, then a free
throw by Spider McHale, their
power forward. And they'd held the

lead—though never a large one—
throughout the first half.

Now, with two minutes and thirty
seconds to go until the break, the
Bulls were behind
by three, 24–21.

MJ heard Jim and
Nate conferring as
Dave brought the
ball up the floor for
the Bulls.

"Brian looks like he's dying out
there," Jim was saying to Nate. "And
besides, he's already got two personal
fouls. Maybe I should give him a
rest?"

Nate looked down the bench.
"Yeah," he answered, "send MJ in for
Brian to finish out the first half. That
way Brian will be fresh for the second
half, and he won't pick up his third
personal."

MJ saw Jim hesitate for a long
time, grimacing. The coach was obviously reluctant to send him into this
close game.

MJ bit his lip and pretended he hadn't noticed Jim's reaction.

"MJ," Jim finally called out, "go on in for Simmons. And no turnovers, please."

Glad you have so much confidence in me, Coach, MJ thought, but he didn't say a word out loud. At the referee's next whistle, he checked in to the game.

It was the Bulls' ball from the sideline in front of their own bench, on their offensive end of the court. Dave inbounded to Jo, who wheeled and threw a hard chest pass to Derek on the right wing.

The instant Derek received the ball, Ratso Renzulli darted over and joined up with Spider McHale to double-team Derek—leaving Will all alone in the pivot!

But Derek didn't see him.

MJ had watched this happen all game. It was the exact same situation MJ had pointed out to Derek at practice, when he and Mark had double-teamed Derek, and Jo had been left open on the perimeter. As awesome a player as Derek was, he just couldn't seem to react quickly to the double-team.

MJ had been tempted to say something to Derek about this from the bench since early in the first quarter, but he'd kept his mouth shut. Now, seeing it up close from out on the floor, it was even more maddening.

With Ratso and Spider all over him, Derek flailed his elbows wildly, attempting to clear some space. MJ wished there was a way he could help his desperate teammate, but this time someone *else* would have to tell him Will was wide open.

Rattled by the flurry of the Slashers' arms and legs, Derek finally let loose a blind heave that missed everything.

Matt Johnstone, the Slashers' red-headed shooting guard, hauled in the air ball and triggered the fast break. Otto made the layup at the other end of the floor, and the Slashers led 26–21.

Derek quickly inbounded to Dave under the Slashers' basket. Dave rushed the ball up the floor and delivered a hard bounce pass to Jo just to the left of the key.

Might as well make myself useful, MJ thought. He set a pick for Jo, and she instantly recognized it. Running Matt Johnstone into MJ's pick, Jo freed herself for the open twelve-footer.

Good!

The Bulls had cut the lead to 26–23. And following a nerve-racking in-and-out miss by Ratso, the Bulls had possession again.

After working the ball patiently around the perimeter, Jo found Derek in the right corner with a nice skip pass over the heads of the Slashers defenders. *Again* Ratso dropped off to double-team him. *Again* Will was left wide open in the paint. And *again* Derek failed to see him.

Get it to Will! MJ was dying to yell out. But he didn't.

He didn't say a word.

"Three seconds!" the referee finally called, pointing his accusing finger at Will. Waiting and waiting for the pass from Derek that never came, Will had stayed in the lane too long and had been whistled for the violation.

The ref handed the ball over to Matt Johnstone along the sideline on the Bulls' end of the floor. But with only four seconds remaining in the half, the best the Slashers could manage was an off-target, thirty-five-foot fling by Otto Meyerson at the buzzer.

The first half ended with the Slashers ahead 26–23.

"We need quicker passes," Nate told the Bulls, punching his left palm with his right fist. "Also, look for the fast break after every defensive rebound. And if you've got an open shot—" Nate flicked his wrist in the classic shooting motion "—take it!"

Jim continued the halftime pep talk, reminding the Bulls to box out, to keep moving their feet on defense, to follow their shots.

This is all very useful information, MJ thought sarcastically, *but does anyone want to mention that when one of your top two players is constantly open six feet from the hoop, it might be a nice idea to get him the ball?*

MJ couldn't believe that neither of the coaches had picked up on the double-team yet. But under the circumstances, *he* sure wasn't going to be the one to bring it up.

No, sir, MJ thought. *Nobody on this team is ever going to hear from me again. Not until they ask.*

The Bulls formed a circle around their coaches, putting their hands in the middle. On Jim's count of three, they chanted, "Show time!"

Just before the starting five headed back onto the floor for the third quarter, MJ heard Will say to Derek, "You know, when Ratso double-teams you, I'm usually wide open in the pivot. Look for me."

Derek nodded.

"Good idea," Jim agreed.

It's about time, MJ thought, shaking his head.

*   *   *

In some ways, the third quarter was more of the same. There was a lot of defensive pressure on both sides of the court and not a whole lot of scoring.

But the Bulls offense looked crisper. With Derek looking to pass when he got double-teamed, the Bulls were able to move the ball a lot more smoothly.

Branford outscored the Slashers 11–7 in the quarter, to take a 34–33 lead. Will accounted for eight of those points, on four baskets.

With a keen sense of satisfaction, MJ noted that *all* of Will's baskets came on passes from Derek after he was double-teamed.

Got to draw first blood this quarter, Will resolved. But instead it was Spider McHale who hit the first hoop of the final period, a running one-hander that put the Slashers up by one.

"Come on, Derek, get a hand in that man's face!" Will heard Mark yell frantically from the Branford bench.

Fortunately, Brian Simmons came right back with a fadeaway jumper for the Bulls.

Then *his* basket was answered by Otto Meyerson, who somehow drove the length of the court through traffic for a layup.

The entire fourth quarter went that way, seesawing back and forth. Neither the Slashers nor the Bulls ever had more than a one-point lead.

"Get that stuff outta here!" Chunky yelled, jumping off the bench as Will ferociously blocked a Ratso Renzulli jumper from close range.

"In your face!" Mark screeched when Derek blew by Spider for a gorgeous reverse layup. Mark pumped his fist in the air triumphantly.

Will could hear the Bulls' bench going ape. Except for MJ. As far as Will could tell, not a word had escaped his lips.

Less than half a minute remained in the game, and the Bulls were up by one. Otto Meyerson controlled the ball at the foul line, but Dave and Jo had him completely bottled up. The best he could do was manage to sneak a desperate pass to Matt in the left corner.

Will thought the shot was well out of Matt's range, but the short, skinny redhead put it up anyway. After bouncing around the rim a few times, the ball dropped through.

45–44, Slashers.

"Come on, guys," Will heard Mark plead hysterically from the sidelines. "Time's running out!"

Will checked the scoreboard clock. Eighteen seconds to go. *Man*, he thought, *we could sure use some words of wisdom from MJ now!*

Seeing that Jim wanted a time-out, Will immediately signaled for one.

The Bulls gathered around their coaches. Will shifted from one foot to the other, back and forth. Brian kept tying and retying the same shoelace. Mark tried to clear his goggles.

Everyone looked tense.

Will knew Jim would set up the play. For all Nate's last-minute, high-school heroics on the court, when it came to coaching, he preferred to leave the crunch-time decisions to Jim.

Jim was a little slow to speak up, Will thought. Usually the moment the team gathered around, Jim had his play figured out and was ready to roll. But this time he hesitated.

With all the Bulls waiting expectantly for him, Jim finally said, "Okay, Will's going to inbound the ball to . . . wait . . . wait . . ."

He seemed to be having second thoughts.

Starting out again, Jim said, "No, *Brian* will inbound to Dave, and . . . no . . ."

Will had never seen Jim so indecisive. The coach just couldn't seem to make up his mind.

Jim clapped his hands. "Okay, here it is, guys. We want Derek to take the last shot. Dave will inbound to Derek. Derek will run behind Will's screen. Hopefully, he'll be open."

By the way Jim had said *hopefully*, Will could tell he wasn't speaking with a lot of confidence. And if ever there was a time confidence was needed, *now* was the time!

Out of the corner of his eye, Will could see Nate turn in MJ's direction. The tall teenager had a searching look on his face.

At the same time, he noticed that Jo and Derek had also turned to MJ. They, too, seemed to be looking to him for help.

It wasn't long before *all* eyes were on MJ.

Will spoke up. "Jim," he ventured, "maybe MJ's got an idea. . . ."

Finally, Jim, too, turned to MJ. "Well?" he asked, shrugging his shoulders. "What do you think, MJ? You have a play ready?"

MJ felt his heart pounding. Did he have a play ready? *Of course* he had a play ready! He *always* had a play ready. All Jim ever had to do was *ask*.

"All right," MJ began, "we definitely want Derek to take the final shot. I agree with that part. But the Slashers always collapse on the man with the ball in pressure situations and forget about everyone else."

MJ was rubbing his hands together as he envisioned the play unfolding. "So let's have Dave inbound the ball to Brian, who'll draw the defense to him. Then he can rotate the ball over to Derek. Derek will be wide open. All he has to do is make the shot."

"Hear that?" Mark laughed, clapping Derek on the back. "Sounds like you've got the easy part. All you've got to do is make the shot."

After one more "Show time!" Will, Derek, Brian, Dave, and Jo took the floor for the Bulls.

The ref handed Dave the ball on the sideline on the Slashers' half of the court.

Otto waved his arms madly in front of Dave's face and jumped up and down as if he were on a pogo stick, but Dave was able to inbound the ball to Brian in spite of Otto's efforts.

So far, so good, MJ thought, holding his breath.

Brian dribbled across half-court, where he was immediately met by three defenders. Sure enough, Derek was wide open in the right corner.

Brian threaded a bullet pass to Derek through the Slashers defense. The Bulls' top shooter squared up, got a good look at the rim, and calmly fired the fifteen-footer as the clock ran down.

Swish!

The Bulls had beaten the Slashers, 46–45.

Mark and Chunky chased the Bulls coaches onto the court, catching first Jim, then Nate, and

emptying a bucket of freezing water on their heads. The rest of the Bulls swarmed Derek, howling and pounding him so hard on the back that the skinny forward toppled over, taking his teammates to the floor with him.

From underneath the tangle of adoring Bulls came Derek's faint voice. "Where's MJ?" he wanted to know.

"Right here," MJ answered. He was somewhere near the top of the pile.

"Hey, good call, man," Derek said softly.

MJ hoped his grin didn't look *too* goofy. All he knew was that he hadn't felt this much a part of the team in weeks.

Then he sensed Jim's hand on his shoulder.

"That's right," the coach said, looking him squarely in the eye. "Good call, MJ."

CHAPTER 9

Mark, as usual, was firing off wise-cracks from his regular seat in the back of the Bullsmobile.

"I never doubted we'd win—not even for a second," he said with a straight face.

The van erupted in laughter. Mark

was well-known for being a total basket case during close games, always thinking the worst was going to happen. MJ knew this as well as anyone, since they often sat side by side on the bench.

"Stop the car!" Dave called out suddenly. "We forgot something!"

"This better be important, Droopy," Nate grumbled as he began to slow the Bullsmobile down.

"It is," Dave said, trying to sound serious. "We forgot to ask the Slashers if they want to come over to Bowman's with us for sodas."

A new round of laughter filled the van. The obnoxious Slashers were notorious around the league for being terrible losers. The idea of Otto, Spider, Matt, and the others sharing sodas and socializing with the Bulls after a tough game was pretty hilarious, MJ had to admit.

"Man, I keep seeing Derek stroking that jumper to win the game for us," Nate said, changing the subject.

Then, eyeing Derek through the rearview mirror, he added, "You looked cool as a cucumber nailing that sucker."

"Hey, I never would have had such a clear shot if MJ hadn't set up Brian as the decoy," Derek said softly.

MJ sat up a little straighter in his seat, proud as could be. Sure, Derek was always modest. But everyone had agreed it was MJ's great call that had allowed Derek to be so open for the game-winning shot.

"How do you always know what's going to work, MJ?" Chunky blurted out. "When we get into crunch time, my mind goes blank."

MJ thought for a moment. "I guess it's just instinct," he began. "Same way Dave can dribble without thinking, or Brian can shoot. I just *see* what should happen. I mean, we all knew Derek was in the zone—"

He felt Dave's eyes on him and his face burned. There he was using that basketball lingo again!

"Oops," MJ excused himself.

"Hey, you can use any of those corny expressions you want," Dave laughed. "Today, you're the man!"

Will, who was sitting in front of Dave, turned around to face him. "A few of us always knew MJ was the man," Will said with a sly smile, "but it seems to me *some* of us here thought MJ was a . . . now what was the expression? A know-it-all?"

MJ knew exactly what Will was getting at. While Will, Derek, Jo, and Nate had been on MJ's side, the rest of the Bulls clearly *had* thought of MJ as a know-it-all. Obviously, Will meant to have a little fun at their expense.

"Isn't that right, Jim?" Will continued, slapping his big brother on the shoulder, the wicked grin still on his face. "I mean, I hate to say I told you so, but—"

"Hey, wait a minute," Jim broke in. "I was *always* happy to listen to what MJ had to say. It was just that . . ."

The end of Jim's sentence was drowned out by the noisiest burst of laughter yet. Nate was shaking so hard he could barely hold the wheel.

MJ knew the Bulls were hysterical not only because Jim had so clearly *not* wanted to listen to him. It was also because one of Jim's best-known weaknesses was his inability to ever admit he'd been wrong.

While the Bulls continued to yuck it up in the back rows of the van, MJ heard Jim and Nate conferring about something up front. The fact that they were whispering gave MJ the impression the subject might be serious.

"All right, settle down," Jim finally called out in what the Bulls sometimes referred to as his "authority" voice. "Nate and I have something we want to talk to you about."

Since the Bulls had been busy horsing around, Jim's sudden change of tone caught them by surprise.

"You know," Jim went on, "lately there've been a bunch of times when

Nate and I can't make it to your practices. We have a lot of stuff going on at the high school, and Nate's got his work at his dad's store. And we hate to leave you goof-offs on your own. . . ."

MJ's heart sunk. *What could Jim be leading up to? And just when I was finally starting to feel comfortable with the Bulls. . . .*

"So we've come to the conclusion," Jim continued, "that we're going to need an assistant around here."

MJ heard several of the Bulls groan at once. The team had already been through a couple of painful experiences involving coaching changes.

"Oh yeah?" Will challenged his brother. "And who's that going to be?"

From his passenger seat in the front of the van, Jim swiveled all the way around to look straight at MJ.

"Let's just call him Assistant Coach Jordan," Jim answered with a great big smile on his face.

MJ felt like he was on a roller

coaster that had gone down a huge drop. *Assistant coach!* That's *exactly* how he'd always wanted to fit in with this team! Sure, playing his few minutes a game was fine—if he didn't screw up too bad. But *coaching!*

Dave shrugged and said, "Good for you, man," as he low-fived MJ's hand. Brian rolled his eyes, but smiled. MJ happily accepted low fives from the rest of the Bulls too.

Then MJ noticed Jim looking at him expectantly. Nate, too, kept glancing at him through the rearview mirror. Clearly he was supposed to say something.

"Thanks!" he blurted out. In his

excited daze, it was all he could think of to say.

"No problem," Nate replied with a wide grin. "Hey, you've been coaching since you came here anyway. Might as well get some credit for it!"

Though he was still in the Bullsmobile, MJ felt like he was floating on top of the clouds.

Assistant Coach Jordan, he thought proudly. *Now that has a nice ring to it!*

Don't miss Super Hoops #13,
Out of Bounds. Coming soon!

There was still one set of hands clapping long after the play had ended. Mark heard his father shout, "Great pass, Mark!"

He's at it again, Mark thought.

Air Ball Archibald brought the ball up slowly for the Panthers. Crossing midcourt, he one-handed the ball over to Graham Duckworth, who'd been waiting just to the right of the key.

Mark lunged to steal the pass, but tripped and fell to the hard floor.

"Good hustle!" he heard his dad yell encouragingly.

Mark scrambled back to his feet and got into a defensive crouch against Duckworth. Mark's face was flushed—with the double embarrassment of falling and having his father *cheer* him for it!

As Duckworth was forced to give up the ball, Mark heard a loud burst of cheering coming from the section where the Bulls' parents were sitting.

"Great stop, Mark! Now *that's* what I call defense!"

It was his father's voice, of course.

About the Author

Hank Herman is a writer and newspaper columnist who lives in Connecticut with his wife, Carol, and their three sons, Matt, Greg, and Robby.

His column, "The Home Team," appears in the *Westport News*. It's about kids, sports, and life in the suburbs.

Although Mr. Herman was formerly the editor in chief of *Health* magazine, he now writes mostly about sports. At one time, he was a tennis teacher, and he has also run the New York City Marathon. He coaches kids' basketball every winter and Little League baseball every spring.

He runs, bicycles, skis, kayaks, and plays tennis and basketball on a regular basis. Mr. Herman admits that he probably spends about as much time playing, coaching, and following sports as he does writing.

Of all sports, basketball is his favorite.